Little, Brown and Company

Hachette Book Group
237 Park Avenue, New York, NY 10017
Visit our website at www.lb-kids.com

LB kids is an imprint of Little, Brown and Company.
The LB kids name and logo are trademarks of Hachette Book Group, Inc.

The publisher is not responsible for websites (or their content) that are not owned by the publisher.

First Edition: May 2013

Library of Congress Control Number: 2013930631

ISBN 978-0-316-23446-7

10 9 8 7 6 5 4 3 2 1

CW

Printed in the United States of America

www.despicable.me

DESPICABLE ME2™

UNDERCOVER SUPER SPIES

Adapted by Kirsten Mayer
Illustrated by Arthur Fong & Christophe Lautrette
Based on the Motion Picture Screenplay
Written by Cinco Paul & Ken Daurio

LITTLE, BROWN & COMPANY
LB kids

There's a villain on the loose! Someone is using a giant magnetic ship to steal a top secret formula from a top secret laboratory!

And it's *so* top secret that only a top secret group of spies knows about it. The spies also know that to catch a villain, you need the help of another villain….

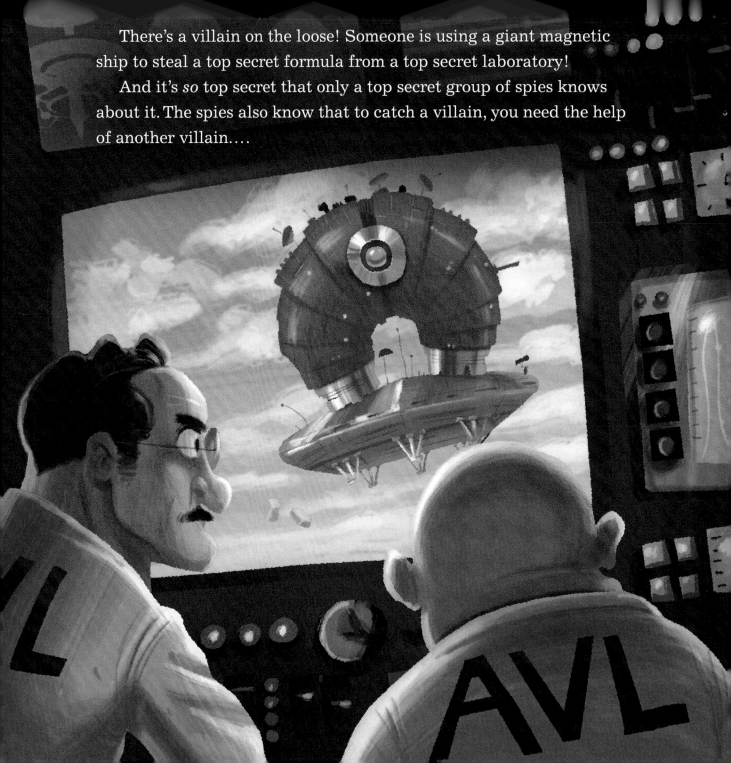

Or, at least, a former villain.

Gru used to be one of the best super villains in the world! He and his army of Minions even stole the moon!

But then he adopted Margo, Edith, and Agnes and became a dad. Now, instead of stealing landmarks, he makes pancakes and blows up unicorn balloons.

One day, while Gru is out walking Kyle the pet, a strange woman approaches him.

"Mr. Gru? Hi! I'm Agent Lucy Wilde of the Anti-Villain League. You're gonna have to come with me."

Gru panics. "Oh, sorry…I, uh…FREEZE RAY!" he yells before grabbing his trusty Ray Gun and sending an icy blast at the stranger. Lucy deflects the attack with a Flamethrower.

"You really should announce your weapons *after* you fire them, Mr. Gru," Lucy says. "For example…" She pauses as she pulls something else out of her purse and suddenly fires at him. *ZAAAAAP!* "AVL-Issued Lipstick!" she cries.

The zapper knocks Gru out long enough for Lucy to drag him into her car and drive off.

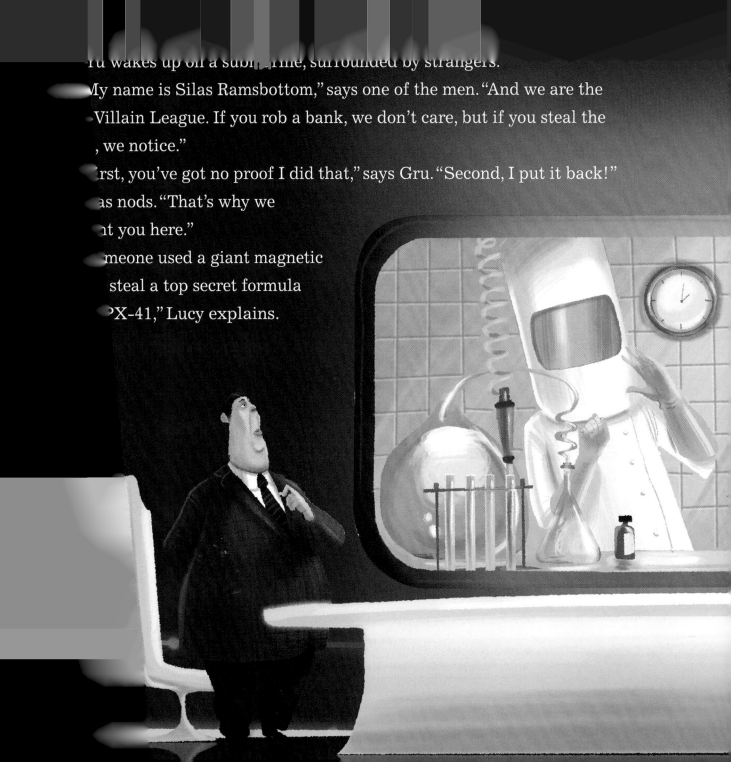

Gru wakes up on a submarine, surrounded by strangers.

"My name is Silas Ramsbottom," says one of the men. "And we are the Anti-Villain League. If you rob a bank, we don't care, but if you steal the moon, we notice."

"First, you've got no proof I did that," says Gru. "Second, I put it back!"

Silas nods. "That's why we brought you here."

"Someone used a giant magnetic to steal a top secret formula called PX-41," Lucy explains.

She plays a video for Gru of a cute little bunny. When it nibbles a bit of PX-41, it turns into a big, furry, purple monster bunny!

"You usually don't see that in bunnies," Gru admits.

"Exactly! PX-41 is a dangerous weapon!" cries Lucy. "And we have found traces of it at the Paradise Mall."

"The mall?!" asks Gru in disbelief.

Silas jumps in. "We need you to go undercover and find it."

Gru gulps. "Um, okay, I guess."

Gru agrees to help the League.

The next day, he goes to the mall disguised as the owner of a cupcake shop called Bake My Day. He and a few Minions are decorating cupcakes when Lucy shows up.

"Hi, partner!" she says, startling Gru.

"What are you doing here?" demands Gru.

"Silas assigned me to work with you. Isn't this great?

Secret spy stuff! This is gonna be fun!" Lucy claps her hands with excitement. "Come on, let's spy on the other stores and find our suspect!"

A giant cupcake on the top of the store entrance has a camera hidden in the cherry. Lucy and Gru have to stand uncomfortably close together to be able to view the hidden video monitor.

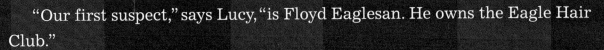

"Our first suspect," says Lucy, "is Floyd Eaglesan. He owns the Eagle Hair Club."

Gru shakes his head. "There's no way that guy is a villain," he states. "His only crime is that wig!"

Lucy shrugs. "Our second suspect is Eduardo Perez, owner of Salsa & Salsa Restaurant. Uh-oh, and he's right here in the shop!"

They bump heads scrambling to greet Eduardo.

"*Buenos días*, my friends!" he says. "Welcome to the mall family! I am throwing a big Cinco de Mayo party, and I need two hundred cupcakes with the Mexican flag on them. I'll pick them up in a week. Okay, bye!"

After he leaves, Gru turns to Lucy. "That's him! He looks exactly like the villain El Macho, but twenty years older. El Macho was ruthless, dangerous, and as his name implies, very macho."

"Then I say we break in to his restaurant tonight after the mall closes to investigate," says Lucy. "It'll be my first break-in!"

That night, after the mall is closed, the two spies sneak back in. Gru is about to kick open the door to Eduardo's Salsa & Salsa Restaurant when Lucy stops him. She takes out her high-tech Nanobot Universal Key that can supposedly open any door. But when that fails to work, she gets frustrated and kicks the door open herself.

Once inside, they hear a clucking sound. They freeze, not wanting to be discovered. "What's that?" asks Lucy. Then a cute little chicken pops out from the kitchen.

But this is no normal chicken. It's a guard chicken!

It flies up to Gru and starts pecking at his bald head! "Get it off me! Get it off me!" cries Gru.

Lucy aims her AVL watch and squirts special foam all over the chicken. The gel quickly hardens into a ball, trapping the bird.

"BAWK!" it objects.

"What is wrong with that chicken?" asks Lucy. "That *pollo*? *Es loco*."

"There's the PX-41! In the safe! I know it!" Gru runs over to the safe and uses a fancy gadget to crack the code. Inside is a glass canister.

"I'm getting pretty good at this job!" he says as he grabs the canister.

"BAWK!" squawks the chicken.

"Someone's coming!" warns Lucy. "Let's go."

They cut a hole in the ceiling with a laser and get out just in time.

They hurry to the Anti-Villain League submarine and wake up Silas. "We found El Macho!" says Gru excitedly. "It's him. Look what we found in his restaurant's safe!"

Silas sticks a spoon in the canister and tastes it.

"No!" cries Gru. "Don't eat that. It's PX-41!"

"That is salsa," declares Silas. "Ripping good salsa at that. Tangy, but with a real kick."

"It's him," insists Gru. "What kind of person puts salsa in a safe? That's weird, right?"

"Mr. Gru, I do not appreciate my time being wasted on a wild-goose chase," scolds Silas. "I'm going back to bed."

"But there wasn't a goose—there was a chicken!" protests Gru.

When Gru delivers the cupcakes to the Cinco de Mayo party, Eduardo greets him with a smile.

"*Mi compadre*, come have some guacamole with me!" he says, leading Gru into an elevator. "I have something planned for you."

During the long elevator ride deep underground, Eduardo says, "I know who you are, Gru. And it's time you know who I really am....I am El Macho."

"Oh! I knew it!" exclaims Gru.

They exit the elevator and enter a huge underground lab.

"I acquired the most powerful substance on Earth with my magnetic ship!" explains El Macho. "How's that for macho? I'm going to use it to create a monster army of creatures that will eat entire cities…and we can do it together!" He claps Gru on the shoulder. "So, are you in?"

"Uh…yeah…probably…I mean, yes! Of course, yes. I just have a lot going on right now…but I am, like, ninety-seven percent in."

"You know what?" El Macho responds. "I am not so convinced that you are in. Let's make sure."

Just then, a rocket rises from steel doors in the ground. Attached to it are a shark, one hundred pounds of dynamite...and Lucy!

"Oh, hey, Gru! Turns out you were right about the whole El Macho thing, huh?" says Lucy.

Thinking fast, Gru grabs a weapon from his pocket and aims it at El Macho.

"I am not afraid of your jelly guns!" the criminal mastermind cries.

"Oh, this ain't no jelly gun, sunshine!" Gru retorts, pulling the trigger and releasing a horrible stinky fart.

The gas knocks El Macho right out! Gru leaps to Lucy's rescue.

Thanks to Gru and his new friends at the Anti-Villain League, El Macho is behind bars and the PX-41 is far from anyone who can misuse it. The world is safe from harm…for now.